For Todd
—Shari

For Mary Beth Malm and Charlie Krucky
—Renée

ACKNOWLEDGMENTS

With appreciation to the Milwaukee County Historical Society, the Milwaukee Public Library,
and MPL librarian Jill Fleck, Business, Technical, and Periodicals Department.
—Shari

Thank you to the Milwaukee County Historical Society
—Renée

✳

SLEEPING BEAR PRESS™

2395 South Huron Parkway, Suite 200, Ann Arbor, MI 48104
www.sleepingbearpress.com © Sleeping Bear Press
Printed and bound in the United States
10 9 8 7 6 5 4 3 2
Library of Congress Cataloging-in-Publication Data
Names: Swanson, Shari, author. | Graef, Renée, illustrator.
Title: Gertie : the darling duck of WWII / written by Shari Swanson ; illustrated by Renée Graef.
Description: Ann Arbor, MI : Sleeping Bear Press, 2023. | Audience: Ages 6-10 |
Summary: "In 1945, against the backdrop of WWII, a
soon-to-be-mama duck builds a nest in a precarious spot in the city of
Milwaukee. Soon, news outlets around the world are carrying the hopeful
story of the plucky duck"-- Provided by publisher.
Identifiers: LCCN 2022036876 | ISBN 9781534111714 (hardcover)
Subjects: LCSH: Gertie (Duck) |
Mallard--Wisconsin--Milwaukee--Biography--Juvenile literature. |
Milwaukee (Wis)--History--20th century--Juvenile literature. |
Human-animal relationships--United States--History--20th century--Juvenile literature.
Classification: LCC QL696.A52 S93 2023 | DDC 598.4/134--dc23/eng/20220803
LC record available at https://lccn.loc.gov/2022036876
Photos: A-20 Bomber: Library of Congress, Prints & Photographs Division, FSA-OWI Collection, [reproduction number, e.g., LC-USF35-1326]
Victory Garden: Library of Congress, Prints & Photographs Division, Farm Security Administration/Office of War Information Black-and-White Negatives.
WPA Poster: Library of Congress, Prints & Photographs Division, WPA Poster Collection, [reproduction number, e.g., [LC-USZC2-1234]

GERTIE

The Darling Duck of WWII

WORDS by **SHARI SWANSON** and PICTURES by **RENÉE GRAEF**

PUBLISHED BY SLEEPING BEAR PRESS™

One April morning in 1945, WHEN THE WORLD WAS WEARY OF WAR, A DUCK FLEW TO THE TOP OF A TALL POST POKING OUT OF THE MILWAUKEE RIVER NEAR A BIG DRAWBRIDGE AND SETTLED IN.

People smiled at the plucky duck nesting on a perch so high above the water in the middle of a busy, noisy city.

"My lands, isn't she cute?" said one woman.

Another wondered out loud, "Now, how in the world . . . ?" They looked from the nest way down to the river below. Even if the eggs somehow hatched, how could the mama duck keep her ducklings safe?

A reporter came to take the duck's picture for the local newspaper. He named her Gertie. Soon he was writing stories about Gertie nearly every day. People came to the bridge just to peer over the railing and catch a glimpse of her.

Gertie seemed to like the crowds. She shook her tail feathers and gave them a glimpse of a bright band around her foot. The people laughed and called it her engagement ring.

Newspapers, filled with bleak articles about the war overseas, now began to include hopeful stories about Gertie. Before long, Gertie stories began to circulate around the world. Even American soldiers overseas read about her and dreamed of picnics, apple pie, and life back home.

As Gertie's fame spread, the crowds watching and reading about her grew.

The bridge tenders announced that they would be the godparents of the future ducklings and kept close watch over Gertie and her nest.

At a time when people worried about the war, everyone hoped that Gertie would be able to succeed in her mission to hatch her eggs safely.

The Memorial Day parade route that year went right past Gertie.

Band after band marched in the streets, but when they got within a block of Gertie on her nest, the musicians hushed and tiptoed across the bridge—all except for one band who played "Rock-a-Bye Baby" for Gertie and her eggs.

Playful Gertie waggled for her fans.
"Look at that gal mug," someone said.

"What if she has 'em during the parade?"
asked one mom with a brood of her own.

"They ought to blow every whistle in town
if she does," said her husband.

Sure enough, Gertie's first egg hatched that night.

As a crowd watched from the bridge, a tiny duckling staggered around outside the nest. The onlookers named him Bill. Gertie struggled to keep Bill under her wing, but he kept pushing his way out, tail first.

Flash news reports about Gertie went out by radio, and the bridge bells clanged. The next day, even more people came to watch Gertie from the bridge.

Bill continued to be a challenge for Gertie. Everyone gasped when Bill tumbled down into the swirling river below. Frantic Gertie didn't know whether to chase after him or stay with her remaining eggs.

The quick-thinking bridge tenders jumped into a rowboat to rescue Bill—after all, he was their godson. But Bill darted away from them, paddling back and forth across the river. Finally, they scooped him up with a long-handled net and deposited him back into the nest.

More eggs hatched that night, but a storm was brewing. When the rain began pouring down, the bridge tenders retreated to their shanty to keep watch. Over and over, the wind blew the little ducklings into the river, and the bridge tenders scrambled out to rescue them.

But the bridge tenders were no match for the fierce wind and storm. Drenched and exhausted, they decided to scoop up all the ducklings, plus one last egg still in the nest, and bring them all into their shanty for safekeeping. Gertie was nowhere to be found.

The bridge tenders didn't know how to save the last little egg. So they called in duck expert Larry Hautz.

The greenish-white egg was cold, but Larry saw a duckling's beak sticking out. He worked all night to free the duckling from the egg, slowly picking away pieces of the shell bit by bit.

Once the duckling was free, Larry rolled it four times in cornmeal to get the moisture out of its feathers. He put the little duckling into his hat and set it by the shanty's stove to keep it warm.

Then the bridge tenders braved the dark storm to search for Gertie. They had no idea where to find the terrified mother. Finally, they spotted her, used some food to lure her into a little box, and brought her back to her ducklings in the warm shanty.

With the little family together again, Larry and the bridge tenders discussed how to keep the ducks safe. They couldn't put the ducks back out into the storm. And even once the storm cleared, their nest was so high that the ducklings could be swept off again into the churning river below.

Larry Hautz had an idea.

The next morning, Gertie and her family greeted their fans from the big picture window of Gimbels department store across the street from their nest.

Word got out, and everyone came by to see Gertie and her "quinducklets": Dee Dee, Freddie, Millie, Pee Wee, and Bill. So many people pressed up against the window that Gimbels had to erect a barrier to keep the glass from breaking.

For three days, the ducklings made their home in the store window. They had fresh water, a sandy floor, and plenty of food. Registered nurses worked around the clock to keep the humidity and temperature just right.

Gertie and her ducklings were safe, but a store window was no place for a duck family.

So, when the weather cleared, Gertie and her five ducklings rode with a police escort to a local park and moved into its lagoon. A joyful parade of fans followed to see them off.

Not long after that, THE WAR WAS WON, AND SOLDIERS CAME HOME TO THEIR FAMILIES. GERTIE RETIRED FROM HER STARRING ROLE ON THE TALL POST IN THE MILWAUKEE RIVER. BUT THE HAPPY STORY OF THE PLUCKY DUCK AND HER DUCKLINGS HELPED LIFT THE SPIRITS OF A WAR-WEARY WORLD, GIVING PEOPLE A REASON TO HOPE FOR A BRIGHTER FUTURE.

MORE TO THE STORY

The events depicted in this story are true. They took place between April 28 and June 4, 1945.

Following the bombing of Pearl Harbor on December 7, 1941, Americans rushed to enlist to help win the war, and millions of women stepped into the workforce, most for the first time. Everyone helped in some way and then gathered around their radios each night to listen to news flashes from the front lines, hoping for peace.

An A-20 bomber being riveted by a woman worker at the Douglas Aircraft Company plant at Long Beach, Calif.

Children were vital contributors to the war effort. Some worked part-time in factories. Others planted, weeded, and harvested Victory Gardens so that the produce their families would normally buy could be sent to soldiers on the battlefronts. Some collected milkweed pods because the fluffy seeds inside could be used in life jackets. Others knitted socks for soldiers. Children across the country responded to President Roosevelt's urging to collect "all sorts of scrap metals, rubber, and rags [to help] turn the tide in the ever-increasing war effort." They gave up their sneakers, balls, and rubber dolls and collected metal and tin, even carefully peeling bits of foil off gum and cigarette wrappers so those things could be recycled into

Guiding hand behind the establishment of many West coast Victory Gardens, Professor Harry Nelson finds time to give his ten-year-old daughter and her Girl Scout friends some pointers in transplanting young vegetables

new products needed in battle. One child in Illinois collected more than one hundred tons of paper and cardboard during the course of the war. Helping in these ways gave the children a "good feeling, a believing in our country and government, a sense of us all pulling together."

At the time Gertie arrived in Milwaukee, Wisconsin, four-term president Franklin Delano Roosevelt had just passed away, and the country was in mourning. The war had lasted years already, with a heavy toll, and people

Poster for the Philadelphia Salvage Committee encouraging scrap drives to aid the war effort.

Gertie the Duck checks out her brood-to-be in a nest formed atop a piling next to the Wisconsin Ave. bridge over the Milwaukee River on May 28, 1945. The story of the duck's unlikely maternity ward captured Milwaukee's attention during World War II. This photo was published in the May 29, 1945, Milwaukee Journal.

longed for something to lift their spirits.

Gertie became that *something*.

Stories about Gertie captured the attention of Milwaukee, the country, and eventually the world. Everyone cheered on the plucky little duck.

Gertie's story was first carried in the *Milwaukee Journal* but was then picked up by other news outlets around the world, including *Stars and Stripes*, a periodical for those in the service. American troops, exhausted and dispirited by the war, were treated to a front-page story about Gertie. One soldier remarked, "Gertie's the greatest morale booster this outfit ever had."

With a worldwide spotlight on Gertie, Milwaukee rose to the challenge of caring for her and keeping her safe. Early on, bridge tender John Stitch said, "Put it in the paper that if anybody in Milwaukee harms one of those eggs, this town ain't fit to live in!" All hands were on deck to protect Gertie. Boy Scout patrols stood guard. A plainclothes Humane Society officer with police powers took over, and even the bridge tenders were deputized with arresting power to protect their duck.

Worried about the long drop to the water from Gertie's nest, Milwaukee officials debated building a ramp and protective screens around the pilings. Concerned about oil in the river water dirtying the ducklings, Milwaukee's flushing station engineers waited on call to flush fresh water into the river at a rate of two and a half million gallons per hour. A fire truck sped to Gertie's nest when a careless onlooker tossed a cigar among her eggs. The bridge tenders floated a raft with corn and grains near her post because the dirty river snaked through concrete walls, and food for a duck was scarce. A project to replace the rotting pilings was delayed because it might upset Gertie. The city even promised that they would issue official birth certificates for the ducklings. Milwaukee's watchword became: "Anything for Gertie."

As a crowd watches on the Wisconsin Ave. bridge, bridgetenders Paul Benn (with skimmer) and George De Grace (at the oars) rescue one of the duck hatchlings, nicknamed Black Bill, after the bird left the nest of its mother, Gertie. The mother duck is in the water just above the rowboat. This photo was published in the June 1, 1945, Milwaukee Journal.

And everyone came to see Gertie as well. Gertie was visited an estimated three million times while she incubated her eggs, and those too far away to visit sent gifts: poems, cards—even diapers. Schools planned field trips to check on Gertie, and streetcars stopped mid-route so passengers could scramble out to see her before continuing on. So many passengers aboard passing boats rushed to see Gertie that the boats tilted in the water.

The *Milwaukee Journal* dedicated four reporters and five photographers to its Gertie coverage, with the Milwaukee radio station flashing hourly bulletins about her. Abroad, military newspapers and radio kept tabs on Gertie. Remarkably, headlines about Gertie shared space with some of the most dramatic turning points in the war. She must have come to her perch not long after President Roosevelt died. As she incubated her eggs, American soldiers and their allies made progress across Europe, pushing back enemies from countries that had fallen and liberating camps where prisoners had been killed or were being kept in inhumane conditions. As readers finally celebrated victory in Europe (VE Day), they also read about all the people making Gertie Mother's Day gifts. And on Memorial Day, with veterans from World War I

Sculptures of Gertie and her ducklings grace the Wisconsin Avenue bridge.

and World War II marching and the newspaper reporting that the American casualties had hit one million people, Gertie's eggs hatched.

Gertie's fame continues. Sculptures of Gertie and her five ducklings decorate the area around the Wisconsin Avenue Bridge. She truly brought joy to the world at a time when people had begun to despair. One journalist said: "And Gertie has taken our minds off some of the ugly things around her; she even helps us forget, for a few minutes, the horrible bungle that man has made of his world."

QUOTATION SOURCES

p. 9.   "My lands . . .": "Duck Hatching Lessons in Life for Her Public." *Milwaukee Journal.* 6 May 1945.

p. 9.   "Now, how in . . .": Ibid.

p. 15. "Look at that gal . . .": "Stage Struck Gertie Wiggles an Encore for Eager Throngs." *Milwaukee Journal.* 30 May 1945.

p. 15. "What if . . .": Ibid.

p. 15. "They ought to . . .": Ibid.

p. 29. "Quinducklets": "IF Day is Good, Quinducklets to Float in the Lagoon Today." *Milwaukee Journal.* 3 June 1945.

TBD   ". . . good feeling.": Whitman, Sylvia. *Children of the World War II Home Front.* Minneapolis: Carolrhoda Books, Inc. 2001. 31. Print.

TBD   "Gertie's the greatest morale booster . . .": Gaskill, Gordon. "The Duck that Will Live Forever," *Rotarian.* August 1961: 36. Print.

TBD   ". . . all sorts of scraps.": Whitman, p. 51.

TBD   "Put it in the paper . . .": "Mallard Sets an Eggs-Ample in a 'Penthouse' 10 Feet Up." *Milwaukee Journal.* 26 Apr. 1945.

TBD   "Anything for Gertie": Gaskill, p. 36. Print.

TBD   "Gertie has taken our minds off . . .": "Since Gertie Came to Town." *Milwaukee Journal.* 7 May 1945.